Five Little Peppers
AND How They Grew

Margaret Sidney's
Five Little Peppers
AND How They Grew

Adapted and Abridged by OLIVE PRICE

Illustrated by CLAUDINE NANKIVEL

GROSSET & DUNLAP • Publishers • NEW YORK

ISBN: 0-448-02239-7 (Trade Edition)

© 1963, by Grosset & Dunlap, Inc.

1976 Printing

The Little Brown House

THE LITTLE Brown House was old. The floors creaked and groaned whenever anyone walked across one of its rooms. But it was really the happiest house! Here eleven-year-old Ben, ten-year-old Polly, and Joel, David and Phronsie, all younger, lived with their mother, whom they called Mamsie. Everyone called them the Five Little Peppers.

"Houses are only as happy as those who live in them," Mrs. Pepper explained to her children. "Even though it is hard to scrape together money enough to put bread in our mouths and to pay the rent, the Little Brown House always knows we are happy just to be together . . . to keep on working and hoping . . . and, often enough, to have fun."

Mrs. Pepper admitted sorrowfully to herself more than once that the Five Little Peppers had not had any bringing up. "They've just *scrambled* up!" she said. And then she would set her lips tightly together and fly at her work faster than ever. "I must get some learning for them some day — some way — but I don't see how!"

It seemed as though there was always something to stop things from going just right. The winter had been very cold. It took so much more to feed and warm the family that the money went faster than ever. And then, when the way seemed clear again, the store where Mrs. Pepper worked got a new owner. She was not given as much sewing to do as with the old owner, and thus did not receive as much payment. Making coats and mending of all kinds was Mrs. Pepper's work. On this all of their lives depended.

Even though less money came in, the Five Little Peppers tried not to notice. They simply worked a little harder. Ben got a job chopping wood for Deacon Blodgett and Polly helped her mother with the sewing that she did have on hand.

One late afternoon Polly and her mother sat sewing by the window. Already it was getting dark. The kitchen was quiet. Even the big black stove was not hissing and crackling as it always did when Polly cooked upon it. The Peppers were taking "a breathing spell." All except Ben, who had not yet come home from his wood-chopping chores.

Little golden-haired Phronsie sat on the floor. She was only three years old. She was watching Joel getting ready to nail a cover on an old box. David was watching him, too.

Brown-haired Polly blinked her eyes. She was finding it hard to see the basting threads she was pulling out of a green cloth coat.

"Oh, dear!" she exclaimed. "I wish we could have as much light as we need, just once!"

Mrs. Pepper was winding threads from the coat onto an empty spool.

"You don't need any light to see these threads," she said quietly. Then she heard a snapping sound. "Take care, Polly. You broke that. Thread costs a lot of money now."

"I couldn't help it, Mamsie," said Polly. "It just seemed to break. And everything costs a lot now, it seems to me!" She picked up a pair of scissors and started to snip as she went on. "But I'd still like some light! About two hundred candles!"

"Two hundred candles!" echoed Joel. "Oh, what a lot!"

And Mrs. Pepper added:

"Goodness, Polly! Two hundred candles all burning at once could set the Little Brown House on fire!"

Phronsie got up from the floor and walked over close to Polly. Standing very still, she looked up at her with big solemn eyes.

"We couldn't let that happen," she said. "We wouldn't have anywhere to go and live."

Suddenly Polly stood up, caught the little girl in her arms, and they spun round and round the old kitchen together.

"Don't you worry, Phronsie," she said. "We'll always take care of the Little Brown House."

But she couldn't help thinking about two hundred candles. She looked at the dingy wooden beams that stretched across the kitchen ceiling, at the darkened walls, at the ugly black stove and the old kitchen table. How two hundred candles would bring them to life with golden glowing light!

Then she glanced at the grandfather's clock in the corner.

"Goodness!" she cried to her mother. "It's almost half past five! It's time for Ben to come home and I'll have to be getting supper!"

Mrs. Pepper folded her sewing and got up from her rocking chair.

"I'll take this into the bedroom, Polly, while you start paring potatoes. Phronsie can help you set the table." Then she spoke to Joel and David. "Put your hammers away now, boys, and fix the kindling wood for Polly."

They gathered things up very slowly. Something was always spoiling their fun, David complained.

Polly pulled the battered table away from the wall into the center of the room. Little Phronsie put a red-checked tablecloth upon it while Polly started bringing dishes from the cupboard. They had only started to lay out the knives and forks and spoons when Ben came into the room.

Phronsie raced into his arms. His face was tingling from being outdoors. His eyes were bright.

"Oh, it's good to be home!" he cried, hugging Phronsie. "Is supper ready, Polly?"

Ben's homecoming was always a big moment in the day for the three younger Peppers. Next to their beloved Mamsie, Ben and Polly were the ones who made the Little Brown House a wonderful home.

And, tonight, at supper, Ben and Polly both had something special to say. Polly said it first:

"Mamsie's birthday will soon be here. If only we could celebrate!"

Mrs. Pepper beamed.

"I don't need a celebration. I have you children and that makes me rich." Then she went on slowly. "If we can only keep together and grow up good so that the Little Brown House won't be ashamed of us, that's all I ask."

Polly looked at Ben and smiled. She waited until supper was over and the kitchen was tidy again to see him alone for a moment.

"I still want to celebrate Mamsie's birthday," she told him.

"But how are we going to do it?" he asked.

"I'm going to bake a big cake," she said. "A big and beautiful birthday cake!"

"She'll see you bake it," Ben told her, "or else she'll smell it."

"No, she won't," said Polly. "Don't you know she'll be out of the house helping Mrs. Henderson tomorrow?"

Suddenly Ben hugged her.

"You think of everything, Polly. You always think of everything!"

The Big Black Witch

MRS. PEPPER left the Little Brown House early the next morning. She planned to work all day for the minister's wife. Ben had to be at Deacon Blodgett's early, too.

Polly watched him go down the walk. Then she hurried back to Phronsie who was standing at the kitchen stove.

"Are we ready to bake the cake now?" Phronsie asked.

Polly ran her fingers through the little girl's golden curls.

"Of course we're ready, Phronsie." Then she looked over Phronsie's head to the big black stove. "If only," she added, "the stove works right and doesn't spit back at us for spite."

"Well, it better not!" declared Phronsie, and shook a little fist at it.

Polly stooped down to the wood box and filled her arms with wood.

"If only we can make it burn," she said, "what a cake we'll bake for Mamsie!"

She got up from her knees. Joel raced forward to help her.

"I'll lift the stove lid, Polly," he said. "Dave filled the wood box with kindling this morning, so it's my turn to help you now."

David was coming across the kitchen. In another moment all four were standing in front of the big black stove, looking at it challengingly.

"I don't know whether to ask it nicely to be a good stove and burn," she said, "or to start scolding it at once."

Phronsie laid her hand on Polly's arm.

"Don't scold it, Polly, and maybe it will be good to us."

"All right, I won't," answered Polly. "I'll just stuff it with wood."

All four held their breath. It was as though they were saying, "Please hurry, Stove. PLEASE BURN!" when suddenly there came the sound of something cracking.

Polly's eyes grew dark with anger. In spite of her promise to "talk nicely" to it, she cried:

"You spiteful old thing! You big black witch! You're spitting out all the putty that Ben stuffed in those open cracks!"

Joel went around the back of the stove to look.

"The cracks are bigger than ever, Polly," he said, "and there's an awful big hole!"

Phronsie had tears in her eyes. Polly was still furious.

"You ugly old witch!" she cried again. "You just couldn't be nice to us, could you?"

"What are we going to do?" asked David.

Polly sighed loudly and looked at the stove. Somehow it seemed to be laughing at her. "What will you do to me now?" it almost seemed to mock.

Little David looked suddenly bright.

"I know something," he said, and without another word he dashed out of the room.

The next moment, it seemed, he was back again. He was carrying an old leather boot top which was his most precious possession. He put it into Polly's hands.

"You can chip this up fine," he said, "and it will fill those cracks."

"So it will," said Polly, patting him on the shoulder. "And what a good boy you are to let us have it!"

After a few moments she started stuffing the leather into the open cracks of the stove. Suddenly Phronsie crowed aloud like a little rooster. The kindling wood was catching fire, giving off gay shooting sparks. The stove was beginning to burn!

Polly looked at it with delight.

"There, now!" she said to the stove. "See that you keep up the good work!"

She walked across the kitchen and took a red shawl off a hook near the kitchen door.

Joel looked at her with surprise.

"Are you going out?" he asked.

Polly shook her head.

"I'm going over to Grandma Bascom's to ask her how to make the cake," she answered. "You and David watch Phronsie."

"Sure we will," said Joel. "I'm going to nail and I've got other things to do."

Polly put the shawl around her shoulders. Then she waved good-by to Phronsie and opened the kitchen door. In another moment she was walking toward Grandma Bascom's.

"Grandma Bascom" wasn't really the children's grandmother. Everybody in the village simply called her by that name. Her cottage was across the lane and just around the corner from the Little Brown House.

Polly skipped along in a hurry and soon came to the little blue door. She didn't stop to knock because Grandma Bascom was deaf and wouldn't hear a knock, anyhow. Polly walked right into the cottage. Grandma was sweeping the floor.

"Well, hello, there, Polly," she said, and smiled. "How's your Mamsie this morning?"

"Pretty well," answered Polly. Then she rattled on. "Tomorrow is her birthday and I want to bake a cake, a big grand cake, to surprise her."

Grandma Bascom heard some of the words, but not quite all.

"Say that again, Polly, please."

Polly walked closer to Grandma and repeated her words.

"Oh, that will be nice, very nice!" said Grandma after she understood.

Then Polly smiled a winning smile.

"But I don't know how to start it, Grandma. I came over to ask you just to tell me how."

A Birthday Cake For Mamsie

GRANDMA BASCOM looked delighted. She was always glad to help Polly.

"So you want to bake a birthday cake!" she said, smiling. "I've got some fine recipes which will tell you how, step by step."

She leaned her broom against the kitchen door. Then she ambled off into the pantry. Soon she was back again.

"I couldn't seem to find the right one," she said. "Come over to the table, Polly, and we'll look through the ones I keep in the teapot."

Polly followed her to the table. She turned the teapot upside down. More than a dozen yellow paper slips tumbled out onto the tablecloths. But search as she would, Grandma Bascom could not seem to find the recipe she was looking for.

"Won't some other recipe do?" Polly asked.

"No, child, no," answered the old lady. "This one is just elegant — light as a feather. It isn't rich, either. No eggs or — "

Polly looked alarmed.

"Oh, I couldn't have eggs!" she cried, blank at the thought of such luxury. "And we have only brown flour, you know."

Grandma Bascom spoke kindly:

"Well, you can make it out of brown flour. The raisins will look even nicer in it."

"Oh, we haven't any raisins!" Polly cried again.

"You haven't any raisins?" Poor Grandma stared at Polly over the rims of her spectacles. "What are you going to put in this cake?"

Polly suddenly seemed hopeful.

"Cinnamon," she said. "We've got plenty of that and it will be good, I guess." Her voice began to sound anxious. "We'll just *have* to use it, Grandma. We just *have* to have a birthday cake!"

Grandma Bascom patted Polly's hand.

"Don't worry. Cinnamon should be all right. Chances are the cake will be good." She walked away from the table and over to the kitchen cupboard. "Now if only I can find that special recipe. Oh, I'm so forgetful!"

It wasn't in the cupboard. It wasn't in the empty sugar bowl, either. It just wasn't anywhere! Polly begged her to give her another one in place of it and she finally did. Then Polly hurried home.

She knew something was wrong the moment she opened the kitchen door. Little Phronsie was curled up in her mother's rocking chair. She was crying bitterly. Joel was trying to comfort her.

"What happened?" cried Polly, racing across the room to Phronsie. Phronsie just cried harder than ever, but Joel explained:

"I was hammering," he said, "and Phronsie's foot got in the way of my hammer."

Polly made Phronsie wiggle her toe to be sure that no bones were broken. As she was "wiggling," the kitchen door opened and Grandma Bascom walked in. She had found the recipe she was looking for and was waving it at Polly.

"Look!" she exclaimed happily. "I found it in my family Bible!" She took a paper bag out of the pocket of her apron. "And I've found some raisins, too!" Then she saw Phronsie's tears. "But what's wrong here? What happened?"

Polly showed her Phronsie's toe. It was turning black and blue. Grandma Bascom decided that it ought to be treated with a certain salve that she had, and she sent Joel to her cottage for it.

"Oh," said Polly, "you're so good! I just can't thank you enough! Even for the raisins!"

While Grandma Bascom treated Phronsie's foot, Polly decided to start mixing the ingredients for the cake. She turned first to Joel.

"Run down and get the cinnamon, will you? It's in the provision room."

The "provision room" was a shed that had been added to the main part of the Little Brown House. It was reached by a short flight of rickety steps, and was called by that name because Polly had said: "It's a good place to keep provisions, even if we haven't any. And it sounds nice!"

"There!" Grandma Bascom was speaking to Phronsie. "You'll soon be hopping around bright as a little bird!" Then she turned to Polly. "I've really got to go now. Good luck with the cake!"

"We'll save you a piece," promised Polly, thanking Grandma again as she walked out.

Joel came up from the provision room with a supply of cinnamon. Polly started mixing batter in a yellow bowl. Carefully she followed Grandma's recipe. Soon the cake was in the oven. All four waited anxiously.

Polly spoke to the stove.

"Be good to us now," she begged it. "This cake is for Mamsie!"

They sat around it a whole half-hour. Suddenly they sniffed.

"Something's burning!" cried David.

Polly opened the oven door.

"The cake's done!" she began. Then she saw something dreadful. "Why — why, it's black on top!"

Quickly she took it out of the oven and set it on the kitchen table. Of all things! Of all bad things! The cake which was to have been so beautiful had a big black crust! And it had fallen down in the middle!

Polly looked at the stove and wailed:

"You *had* to be a big black witch! You just *had* to be, didn't you? Now you've spoiled our Mamsie's birthday cake!"

Suddenly a cheerful voice was speaking right behind her.

"Don't be too sure, Polly," it said.

Polly turned to see a neighbor, Mrs. Beebe. She was the friendly shoemaker's wife.

"But — " said Polly. Then her voice broke.

Mrs. Beebe thrust a small bunch of golden jonquils into Polly's hands. They had been the first flowers to bloom in her garden this year.

"Take these," she said quietly, "and put them on top of that cake. They will hide the black part."

"Let's see," said Polly, wiping her eyes.

She arranged the flowers in the hollow of the cake. Suddenly it seemed to wear a crown of gold! All four little Peppers smiled.

"It's beautiful! Oh, it's beautiful!" cried Polly, and hugged Mrs. Beebe.

And it was just as beautiful when they set the table for their Mamsie's birthday. When she came in and saw it decked with flowers, she thought it the most beautiful cake in all the world!

"Happy Birthday, Mamsie!" Ben sang the words like a song. The other four Peppers joined him.

Even the big black stove seemed to beam on them all.

Trouble

JOEL pushed his chair back from the table and scowled.

"Mush and molasses for breakfast again!" he grumbled. "Wish we could have something new once."

"Better be glad you've got that," Mrs. Pepper scolded. "Folks shouldn't complain as long as they've got something to eat."

But Joel scowled again.

"I'm tired of the same old things," he said. "Pretty soon I'll be turning into a meal bag or maybe a molasses jug!"

Little Phronsie giggled at the very thought of Joel turning into a jug of molasses. But Ben had a hard day's work before him and he was hungry. He reached out to pick up Joel's plate.

"I'll eat it for you," he said. "I think it's better than nothing."

Joel looked suddenly alarmed. He moved his plate out from Ben's reach and took a big mouthful of mush.

Meanwhile, Mrs. Pepper said:

"Now for our plans for the day. You needn't help me sew this morning, Polly. I want you to run down to the parson's and see how he is."

"Is he sick?" asked Polly, surprised.

"He was taken with a chill, Miss Fulsom told me last night. By now he may have a fever."

Polly got up from the table.

"I'd better go right away," she said. Then she looked at Phronsie. "Want to come with me?" Suddenly she laughed. "Well, I guess you don't. Funny, you're fast asleep!"

Polly went quietly out of the Little Brown House. She skipped along the pebbled path that led up to the minister's house with its old-fashioned green door. She hoped that Miss Jerusha, the minister's sister, would not answer her knock. She had never liked her much. She was a big woman with sharp black eyes and spectacles.

Polly waited a moment after she had knocked. She heard a scuffling sound inside the house. Then the door swung open and Miss Jerusha stood there. Polly felt confused. She had told her mother once that Miss Jerusha always made her feel as if she didn't even know what her own name was!

"Good morning," Polly managed to say politely.

"Well, what do you want?" asked Miss Jerusha as though she had never seen her before.

"I came to see — my ma sent me — " Polly stammered.

"Who is your ma?" asked Miss Jerusha. She spoke like a policeman.

"I live in Primrose Lane," said Polly. Then suddenly a gentle voice was heard inside the hall.

"It's Polly Pepper, Jerusha," it said. "Come right in, my child."

Polly smiled happily. She had always liked the minister's wife, Mrs. Henderson. And right in back of her stood the minister, smiling, too.

"Oh," said Polly, looking up at him, pleased, "you are not going to have a fever and be sick and die."

"I just won't have it, Polly," he laughed. "I'm feeling fit as a fiddle!"

She gave him her mother's message which she now easily remembered. Before either Mrs. Henderson or the minister could answer, Miss Jerusha said:

"There! A cat couldn't sneeze in this town but everybody would know it in a quarter of an hour!"

But Mrs. Henderson took Polly's hand and smiled.

"Let me show you my new chicks. They're all downy golden feathers!"

Polly picked one up in her hands. It started to chirp, and when she snuggled it against her, it chirped even louder. By that time the mother hen was scolding and so Polly put it tenderly back into the box. It ran as fast as it could to get under its mother's wing.

"The darlings! Oh, the darlings!" cried Polly.

Mrs. Henderson smiled.

"Wait a moment, Polly," she said. "My sister sent me some nice country butter and I want to share it with your mother. Will you take it home for me?"

Indeed Polly would! As she carried it up the path that led to the Little Brown House, she was thinking, "If Phronsie's awake, I'll give her some bread with lots of this good butter."

But as soon as she opened the door and walked into the kitchen, Polly knew that something was wrong. Mrs. Pepper sat in her rocking chair. She was holding Phronsie in her arms.

"What's the trouble, Mamsie?" she asked.

"I don't know what it is, Polly, but Phronsie's got a fever. You'll have to go for the doctor just as fast as you can."

Phronsie sick! Polly stared at her hard. Then she set the bowl of butter on the table.

"I'll run all the way to Dr. Fisher's," she promised.

Soon Dr. Fisher was looking at Phronsie.

"It's measles," he said. "That's all. No cause for alarm now."

So Phronsie would get better. But before she did, she passed the measles on to Ben. For days and days and days there was sickness in the Little Brown House. Polly was chief nurse, of course. Young David and Joel tried to carry on Ben's work at Deacon Blodgett's.

Then, just as the sickness seemed to be over, something happened that seemed even worse.

One day, Polly was trying to sew.

"Oh, dear," she thought, "I wonder now what ails my eyes? They feel as though they're full of sand."

She rubbed and rubbed them while her mother wasn't looking. She wouldn't want to worry Mamsie! For a moment they felt better, but then they both began to pain. She closed her eyes for a moment and the pain went away. Then she started to sew again.

"There, now!" she said a moment later. "Who says I can't do it?" Then she looked at her mother. "I think I can finish this tomorrow!"

Mrs. Pepper looked pleased.

"Fine, Polly!" she said. "If you can do that, you'll be the greatest help yet."

But the next day the pain in her eyes was even worse than it had been. Then she looked into the mirror and saw red spots on her face.

"I've got the measles, too," she moaned, "and my eyes — oh, my eyes!"

She scarcely saw Joel as he came into the kitchen.

"Hello," he said. Then, as he saw her staring into the old cracked looking glass, he asked, "Why, what's the matter, Polly?"

She turned around to look at him, but she could not see him clearly. In another moment she just could not see at all! Trembling all over, poor Polly suddenly wavered. Then she fell in a heap on the floor.

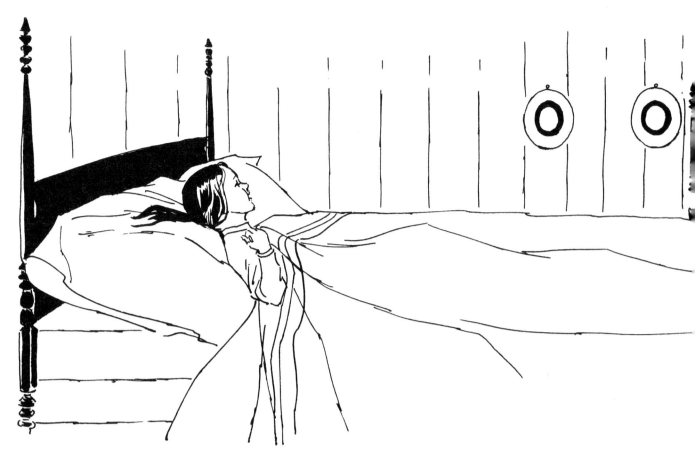

Shadows Over Polly

POLLY lay on her bed while poor Mrs. Pepper bandaged her eyes with an old soft handkerchief. Suddenly Polly seized her hand.

"Don't you worry about me, Mamsie," she pleaded. "I'll be all right."

Mamsie's bright eyes filled with tears.

"That's just like you, Polly," she said very tenderly. "Always thinking of me and the others. Now it's our turn to think of you. When Dr. Fisher comes —"

A voice from the hall broke in upon hers.

"I'm here, Mrs. Pepper," said Dr. Fisher. "Now, what seems to be wrong with Polly?"

Mrs. Pepper turned to him gratefully.

"Oh, thank heaven for you, doctor!" she said. As he walked toward the bed, she murmured, "She has measles, I know, but there's something wrong with her eyes, too."

"Her eyes!" said Dr. Fisher. "What has she been doing?"

Mrs. Pepper's voice was tragic.

"Sewing too much," she answered. "But Polly does everything, Dr. Fisher. We just can't get along without her."

26

The doctor moved close to Polly and took a long time examining her. Finally he stood up straight.

"Well, Mrs. Pepper," he said, "you'll all have to get along without Polly for a spell. Her eyes are very bad."

Dr. Fisher opened his black bag and took out a small bottle.

"Let's see if this won't help," he said.

He put a cooling lotion drop by drop into Polly's eyes. She had expected that it would make her eyes feel cool at once, but it didn't. Even after Dr. Fisher had put a new bandage over them, they still hurt and felt hot.

After Dr. Fisher left, Grandma Bascom knocked on the door of the Little Brown House. Mrs. Pepper answered it.

"You must be having trouble," Grandma Bascom said softly. "I just saw Dr. Fisher leave."

Dear, deaf Grandma Bascom! Mrs. Pepper grasped her hand.

After Grandma helped with the chores, she took Joel home to her cottage. She had said that she had peppermints and wanted the Peppers to have them. Peppermints! Joel would walk a mile for them! He followed her into what she called her "keeping room." He watched her open a chest of drawers and take out a paper bag.

"Here they are," said Grandma. "Aren't they pretty? Now you take these home to the sick ones. Peppermints are good for little patients."

Joel could not resist popping one into his mouth first. Then he ran all the way back to the Little Brown House and passed them all around.

It seemed a long, long time until Polly even started to feel better. Day after day she lay in a room that had to be darkened so that not even a crack of light could come through the bandages over her eyes. Sometimes she sat up in the big rocking chair. And Polly hated doing nothing! She was used to bustling around and doing things for others.

Dr. Fisher came and went to the Little Brown House. He even took Phronsie for rides in his carriage. The first time that she went, Polly was allowed to come to the kitchen door to see them off. Of course, she couldn't see because her eyes were bandaged, but she could hear their excited voices. She, too, called to them gaily:

"Sit up straight and pretty, Phronsie! It isn't every little girl who can ride with Dr. Fisher!"

And so Phronsie did sit straight. And she looked very pretty, indeed, in her flowered bonnet.

This event made all the Peppers feel happy, but that very day they were plunged into gloom again. This time it was caused by Joel. Never — no, never — had anyone gotten sick so suddenly in the Little Brown House! He was delirious! Joel, who had always seemed the healthiest one of them all!

"Mamsie, oh, Mamsie!" Polly and Mrs. Pepper huddled forlornly together.

"Don't cry, Polly! Please don't cry!" Mamsie begged her softly. "Tears will only hurt your eyes and make them worse!"

"But Joel may even die!" cried Polly, weeping even harder. "Everybody's sick now and you're all alone and you need my help!"

"Please, Polly, please!" Mamsie spoke in alarm.

But Polly was not to be stopped. Someone had to help Mamsie!

"I don't care if I do go blind — I've just got to help you!" she cried.

Then she did the worst thing she could possibly do. Polly tore the bandages off her eyes.

The Organg Grinder

WHEN Dr. Fisher came to see Joel, he heard what Polly had done. He shook his finger at her sternly.

"Polly!" he scolded. "Polly Pepper! No matter what happens to Joel, you've got to keep those eyes covered! And dry those tears!"

So Polly had to stop crying. She couldn't even see Dr. Fisher draw her mother into a corner. Nor could she hear him talk to her in whispers. Then, less than a week later, something happened.

Joel sat up in bed and cried:

"I want something to eat!"

"Thank the Lord!" cried Mrs. Pepper. "He's going to be all right."

From that moment on, things in the Little Brown House took a turn for the better. Joel had always been so healthy before this sudden sickness that he seemed to get well in no time. And then there came a day, a big day for them all. Dr. Fisher said that Polly's eyes were well enough to have the bandages removed for good!

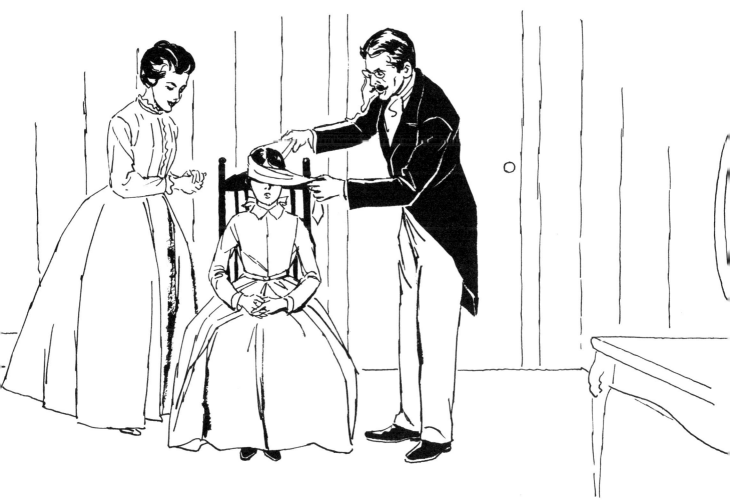

It was a solemn moment for Mamsie and the Five Little Peppers. They stood in the bedroom and watched while Dr. Fisher looked at her eyes.

"Blink, now, Polly. Blink!" he ordered.

Polly opened and closed her eyelids.

"Now," he said, "open your eyes wide!"

Polly did as he told her. Then suddenly she cried with happiness.

"Oh, dear Dr. Fisher," she said, "my eyes are just as good as new!"

The Peppers all gathered around her, hugging her so hard it was a wonder she wasn't crushed, as Ben said very happily. Suddenly it seemed that the Little Brown House wanted to turn inside out with joy.

And after Dr. Fisher left, Polly decided that she wanted to burn up her bandages. She started toward the kitchen, but Ben held her back.

"Wait a moment, Polly," he said.

"But why?" she asked, puzzled.

Then Mamsie's voice came from the kitchen.

"She needn't wait any longer, Ben. Everything is ready now."

Four little Peppers led Polly out into the big warm kitchen. And there stood a surprise!

"Oh!" Polly looked and stood stock-still. "Oh!" she repeated again with delight. "The big black witch is gone! We've got a new stove!"

This had been a secret they had all kept from her. Ever since the day Dr. Fisher had drawn Mamsie into that corner and talked to her in whispers, they had all known that the big black witch was going to go. He and Mamsie had arranged for this new stove to be a surprise for Polly when her eyes were better.

And now the great day had come. This stove was black, too, but it shone like ebony, and somehow seemed to smile. It had a big oven.

"Almost big enough for me to crawl into!" Little Phronsie crowed.

Even the oven seemed to say, "I'm going to make sunshine in this house!"

Then they all took hold of each other's hands and danced around it.

"We are never going to have any more burnt bread," Polly promised them gaily. "Oh, I wish Dr. Fisher could have seen it today!"

Mrs. Pepper laughed.

"He's already seen it, Polly. But you haven't asked where the stove came from."

Polly had been so overwhelmed that if the stove had really dropped from the clouds, it would not have astonished her, as long as it was here. That was the main thing. But now she was saying:

"Surely Dr. Fisher didn't bring it, Mamsie?"

Mrs. Pepper laughed again.

"He didn't exactly bring it, but I guess he knew something about it."

"Oh, he's the splendidest man!" breathed Polly. "Did he really get it for us?"

Mrs. Pepper spoke quietly.

"Yes," she said, "he did. I couldn't stop him. I don't know how he found out you wanted a new stove so much, but he said it must be kept for a surprise for you when your eyes got well."

Polly's voice almost broke with gratitude.

"Oh, bless him, Mamsie! Bless him!" Then she added gaily, "The first thing that I bake in that oven will be apple tarts for Dr. Fisher!"

So all was happy in the Little Brown House as week after week went by. Then there came a dark day, indeed. The Five Little Peppers would never forget it.

Phronsie was sitting under the apple tree in the yard. She was playing with her rag doll. Polly was hanging up clothes on a wash line nearby.

Then suddenly it came — the sound of merry music! It was being played by an organ grinder just beyond the picket fence. Phronsie looked up, enchanted. Oh, it was lovely to hear such music! And the organ grinder looked very gay as he turned the big crank round and round.

Suddenly something jumped up on the fence. It was a small animal! And it had brown fur! Phronsie had never seen a monkey.

The organ grinder told Phronsie that the monkey's name was Jocko. Then he pulled a string and struck up another merry tune. Phronsie clapped her hands in delight as the monkey started to hop about.

The monkey was wearing a little red hat. He took it off and bowed to Phronsie. Oh, never had she seen anything she liked so much!

Mrs. Pepper came out of the house with slices of brown bread and potatoes in her hand.

"I can't pay you," she said to the organ grinder, "but I can give you something to eat."

Suddenly he looked very annoyed.

"Haven't you anything better'n that?" he grumbled.

Poor Mrs. Pepper looked sorry.

"It's just the best we have," she answered.

The man threw the bread down on to the road as he turned away. Little Jocko was not so choosy. He ran around and snapped it up before he followed his master.

Phronsie was almost in tears.

"Oh, I liked them," she cried. "I really liked them! I wish they would have stayed!"

Polly tried to comfort her before she followed her mother into the house.

"Another monkey will come one day," she told Phronsie.

But even though Polly and Mrs. Pepper went back to work in the kitchen, Phronsie still stood and looked after Jocko.

About two hours later, Polly said merrily:

"I'm going to call Phronsie in, Mamsie. She must be tired and hungry by this time." She went to the kitchen door and called, "Phronsie!"

But there was no one there. Phronsie wasn't anywhere. Not on the road. Not at the fence. Not even under the apple tree.

Only her rag doll lay face downward on the grass. Polly was almost wild with fright. That organ grinder! And he had been angry.

ANGRY ENOUGH TO TAKE PHRONSIE WITH HIM!

Jasper

SOON everyone in the village knew that little Phronsie Pepper had been taken away by "an organ man and an awful monkey." Many had come to the Little Brown House after they had helped Ben search the village, street by street. They were gathered in the kitchen.

"We will have to search *all* roads," Ben said firmly. "One of us must take the stagecoach to Boxville. I'll take Deacon Brown's wagon along the Hingham road, and somebody else must go to Toad Hollow."

"I'll go on the stage," said Joel, who had cried so much that he could scarcely see out of his eyes. "I'll find her, I will."

Ben looked at him kindly.

"Be quick, then, and catch the stagecoach at the corner."

Joel was on the stagecoach in no time. He sat on a seat next to an elderly gentleman. And he was so anxious to see both sides of the road at once that he knocked off the old gentleman's hat bobbing up and down. Seeing the stranger was ready to sputter, he explained:

"My sister's been taken off by a man with a monkey," he said, "and she's only three years old." Suddenly he caught sight of something pink he thought might be Phronsie's apron. "There she is!" he shouted.

The driver of the stagecoach had had his instructions. He, too, wanted to find little golden-haired Phronsie. He brought the stage to a stop at once.

But when they got up to it, Joel saw that it was only a bit of pink calico flapping on a clothesline. He climbed back into the coach.

The others were having no better luck than Joel. No one was finding Phronsie. To eleven-year-old Ben, who was driving Deacon Brown's wagon toward Hingham, the minutes seemed like hours. On and on he went. Suddenly the horse stopped. Ben started to snap the reins to make him move on, when — what was that over there in a thicket?

The horse waited quietly while Ben climbed down from the wagon. He raced to a patch of scrubby bushes on a hill beside the road. There he saw a little bundle and close beside it, a big black dog. Standing guard over both was a boy a little bigger than Ben. He had honest gray eyes. And the bundle on the ground was Phronsie!

"Don't wake her up!" the boy warned as Ben leaped up the hill.

"She's my sister!" cried Ben. "Our Phronsie!"

"Maybe she is," the boy said kindly, "but I wouldn't wake her yet if I were you."

He reached out to take Ben's hand.

"My name is Jasper," he said. "I'm spending the summer in Hingham with my father."

"My name is Ben," said Ben, returning the handshake.

Ben was about to move closer to his little sister when the big black dog growled. It looked like a police dog. And when it started to show its teeth, Ben took no more chances. He just stood stock-still.

Jasper spoke to the dog.

"It's all right, Prince," he said, laying a hand on its head. "This is the little girl's brother." He turned back to Ben. "Prince would guard her with his life," he added.

"Good, wonderful dog!" Ben couldn't help saying.

Then flinging himself down on the grass, Jasper told Ben how he had come to rescue Phronsie.

"Prince and I were out for a walk," he explained. "We were about a mile away from here. All of a sudden, I saw a man with an organ and a monkey — and a very tired-looking little girl was beside them."

"Poor little Phronsie!" Ben's voice was low.

"The little girl was crying," Jasper went on, "and as soon as Prince saw that, he growled. The man turned and saw us. He looked so mean and cringing that I knew something was wrong. I asked him what he was doing with a little girl like that."

"You were brave to question him," said Ben.

Jasper's eyes darkened.

"Before he could answer," he went on, "the little girl screamed, 'I want Polly!' Then the man tried to hit her and Prince got busy at once! While I tried to topple him over, Prince went at him and kept at him and bit him until the man had to run as fast as he could!"

Ben couldn't help but reach out to pet the dog.

"Thank you, Prince. Thank you," he murmured. Then he said to Jasper. "I know Phronsie was frightened."

Jasper looked at the child with affection.

"Not a bit," he said cheerfully. "She just clung to me like everything. I wish she were my little sister," he added impulsively.

Ben looked at him steadily.

"I'm certainly glad that it was you who found her, Jasper. And now, I'll have to take her home."

Jasper suddenly grinned.

"May I come to see you sometime?" he asked.

"I want you to," said Ben. "Mother and Polly will want to meet you, too. We'll just never be able to thank you enough."

Then, without waking her up, they put Phronsie up on the wagon seat. The next thing that she knew, she was hearing Mamsie's voice:

"Phronsie! Thank God!"

A Whole New World

IT WAS only a few days later that Jasper and his dog came to visit the Little Brown House. Ben was piling up logs in the yard when he heard a boy's voice beyond the fence.

"Hello, Ben," it said.

Then Prince, too, said "hello" with a bark.

Ben's face was joyful as he raced toward Jasper.

"Oh, you've come! I'm so glad to see you! Polly will be glad to see you, too."

But Polly had been at the kitchen window and was already in the doorway. Ben called to her proudly.

"Come on out, Polly. This is Jasper!"

"Wonderful!" cried Polly, racing to meet him with outstretched hands.

"And this is Prince."

Polly knelt down beside the dog. Unusually enough, he immediately laid his dark furry head in her lap.

"I love you, Prince," said Polly. "You and Jasper saved our Phronsie."

She led them into the big kitchen. Jasper looked around, delighted. He had never been in a kitchen like this before. Where he lived there were servants — cooks and butlers and cleaning women — but here was a family, a devoted family, having fun!

"Hello!" cried the Five Little Peppers. "We're so happy to meet you!"

Phronsie tugged at Jasper's sleeve.

"Come see our new stove," she said proudly. "Polly's baking biscuits, so you had better stay and eat with us."

Jasper looked delighted. What fun it would be to eat in this kitchen! At home he was always served in a formal dining room. Meanwhile, David was asking:

"Where do you live in Hingham, Jasper?"

The boy's face clouded.

"I don't really live there. My father and I are staying at the hotel. He hasn't been very well. He thought a summer here would do him some good."

"But where is your mother?" asked Polly.

"I haven't any mother," he answered quietly.

No mother! For the life of her, Polly couldn't imagine how anybody could feel without a mother.

"You must come out here and share our Mamsie with us," she said softly. "We just can't do enough for you after you saved Phronsie for us."

"Share your Mamsie!" a bright voice echoed. There stood Mrs. Pepper at the kitchen door.

When she heard Jasper's story, she wanted to gather him into her arms along with her Five Little Peppers.

But his life had a pleasant side, too, he told them. He lived in a stately old house in the city. His father had servants to run it. Best of all, there was Marian, his father's sister, and her three sons, Dick, Van, and Percy, who were his cousins. They often came to the big house to visit, so he really had some kin, even if they weren't brothers.

"The big house must be beautiful," said Polly.

Jasper only shrugged.

"I guess it is," he said slowly. Then his eyes shone as he looked around the kitchen. He smiled as he sniffed biscuits browning. "But this," he went on, "is more real!"

Polly went to the stove to take the biscuits out of the oven. Mamsie straightened the red-and-white checkered tablecloth.

"Sit down and have some buttered biscuits with us," she said to Jasper, smiling. "And, remember, you have really two families now—a home with your father and cousins, back in that big house, and another home here, with the Five Little Peppers."

That made Jasper so happy he could have cried, but he bit into a biscuit instead.

"Oh, how good this is!" he murmured, and looked gratefully at Polly.

So that was the beginning. Getting to know Jasper seemed to open up a bright new world for the Five Little Peppers. All summer long he came to see them and there were wonderful days for them all. They went swimming in Toad Hollow. They trudged back and forth to the village. They swung from branches on the apple tree.

Jasper even learned to help the children with their chores. He chopped kindling wood with Ben. He went to the store and carried home "orders" with David and Joel. He fetched and carried for Polly, and he fixed Phronsie's doll. Yes, it was a different summer than he had ever known. He couldn't begin to say how much it meant to him. He could only whisper in Prince's ear:

"Isn't this wonderful, Prince?"

And Prince wagged his tail happily because for him, too, it was the best summer he had ever known. He was always the children's faithful companion. As he had done that first day for Phronsie, he would protect them all with his life, if necessary.

Presently there came a day when the Five Little Peppers met Jasper's father. And although they did not know it then, it marked a turning point in their lives.

Christmas Bells

THE Five Little Peppers didn't know it was really the gingerbread boy that brought Mr. King to the Little Brown House. They had baked it for him because he was sick and sent it to his hotel in Hingham.

Now Jasper King, as everyone knew, was a cantankerous man. All his life he had had what he wanted. If things didn't go as he wanted them to, he was likely to storm about and find out the reason why. And things had not been going right in Hingham. He didn't feel any better there than he had felt at home. He had just as many ailments.

When Jasper gave him the gingerbread boy, it had made him laugh. Phronsie had made the eyes and ears out of pink icing, and she had put them on crooked, which made the figure quite comical.

Mr. King had held it in his hands as he sat at his writing table.

"Ho, ho!" he had laughed. "A gingerbread boy! I haven't seen one since I was a boy! Whoever made him so crooked?"

"Phronsie," Young Jasper had told him.

Mr. King had laughed again and put it on the table in front of him.

"He looks too good to eat," he had roared. "I'm going to keep him here to make me remember how wonderful a gingerbread boy made me feel when I was as young as you are." Suddenly he, too, had looked droll. "Maybe I'd better go see this Phronsie."

"Oh, would you, Father?" Jasper had cried. "She's only three years old and she'd love you!"

So one day, the last of September, a carriage drove up to the Little Brown House. Mrs. Pepper saw it first.

"Oh!" she turned to the family, aflutter. "I think we're having a visitor. It must be Jasper's father."

Polly fairly flew to the kitchen door.

"Jasper!" she called back over her shoulder. "Come out here and see!"

The boy had been playing checkers with Joel who was suddenly so excited that he almost upset the checkerboard. By that time Jasper's father was already greeting Polly at the door.

"Is this little Miss Pepper?" he asked.

Polly had never been called *that* before!

"I don't know, sir," she answered. "I'm Polly Pepper."

"Is your mother in?" asked the old gentleman who was so tall he could scarcely enter the low doorway.

Mrs. Pepper came forward with a warm smile.

"How nice of you to come!" she said. "Do come in and have a cup of tea with us."

Phronsie rushed out from behind a kitchen chair.

"I'm Phronsie," she told him, her pretty eyes shining. "Your Jasper saved my life!"

"Humph!" said the old gentleman, but he looked at Jasper moving toward him and there was pride in his eyes.

There was no more ceremony. The Five Little Peppers welcomed him as if he had always been one of the family. Phronsie crawled up on his lap and nestled her golden head against his broad shoulder. Dignified Jasper King had never seen such a friendly place as this shabby kitchen!

When Mrs. Pepper poured tea he said:

"I should have come here sooner. This is the nicest thing that has happened to me since I've been in Hingham."

Mamsie spoke softly.

"We almost feel now that Jasper is our own. We shall never be able to thank him enough for saving Phronsie from the awful organ grinder."

Jasper's father looked at her glowing face.

"You have already more than thanked him," he said. "He hasn't been so happy all this summer." Then he went on slowly. "It is a pity that we have to leave here tomorrow."

"Tomorrow!" All spoke at once. All voices were shocked.

Mr. King nodded.

"I received a telegram this morning that I must be in the city on Thursday. And besides," he said to Mrs. Pepper, "I think this climate is bad for me now because I have more rheumatism."

Mrs. Pepper looked sympathetic.

"We're all so sorry, so very sorry," she said.

Polly looked at Jasper, downcast.

"Now we can't study music together. Mrs. Henderson was going to let me practice on the piano in the Sunday School room." She turned to face Jasper's father. "I just love music!" she said, her face aglow.

Little Phronsie was in tears.

"I'll miss Jasper so much," she whimpered. Then she looked up at Mr. King, her baby face sorrowful. "And now I'll miss *you!*" she added.

Suddenly Mr. King hugged her as he hadn't hugged a little girl in many years. No one could resist golden-haired Phronsie! But there was no more time. He stood up to go. For a moment he put his hand nervously into his pocket, but when he glanced at Mrs. Pepper's eyes, he drew it out again.

"No, it wouldn't do," he said to himself. "She isn't the kind of woman to whom one could offer money. I'll have to find another way."

And since he always got what he wanted, Mr. King did find a way to make the Five Little Peppers happy.

Although he and Jasper left Hingham the very next day, he was even then looking forward to Christmas!

What he did not know was that the family in the Little Brown House had never had a real Christmas. *Never*. There had never been enough money, or even things, to celebrate with. But this year, thanks to Jasper's

father, it was the loveliest, merriest Christmas that the Five Little Peppers could possibly have had.

Gifts were piled against the tree like snowflakes! There were many things for everyone.

There was a lovely blue scarf for Mamsie. Polly unwrapped books from Jasper with a note that read: "We'll read them together again next summer."

There were skates and games and fishing poles for young Joel and David, a warm woolen coat for Ben, and for little Phronsie, a beautiful wax doll in a pink silk dress! Upon it was a note: "For Phronsie, from one who enjoyed her gingerbread boy."

Then Polly spied another package with a note that said: "For Miss Polly Pepper, to give her music every day of the year."

The package wasn't completely wrapped. Two tiny eyes peered out at her. She was greeted with a song!

"Mamsie!" she cried. "Oh, wonderful! A little bird for my very own! A darling little yellow bird!"

Polly went to the kitchen window. Snow was falling in large white flakes. The sound of bells came from the church steeple.

"This is a *forever* Christmas," she told herself happily as she stood alone in the candlelight. "The one I'll never, *never* forget."

Polly Goes Away

POLLY decided to call her singing bird, Cherry. Sometimes she fed him crumbs from her hand, just to see how adorable he looked. The Little Brown House had always been happy, but now that it had a singing bird it seemed happier than ever.

Then, shortly after Christmas, there came another surprise — Mr. Henderson, the minister, offered to teach Ben "book learning." This seemed wonderful, indeed, because as Mrs. Pepper said, "There's nothing like book learning, Polly. Nothing like it in this world."

"Oh, dear!" said Polly, sewing nearby.

"What is it?" asked Mamsie, seeing Polly looking troubled.

"Why," began Polly, and then finished very slowly, "I shan't know anything and Ben will be ashamed of me."

"Yes, you will," said Mrs. Pepper. "You just keep on trying and the Lord will send a way."

And so it seemed a few weeks later. A letter came from the city — not from Jasper, but from Mr. King. He invited Polly to come to his

house and live with his family. Jasper, Mr. King's sister, and her boys wanted her to come, too.

"Live with them!" cried Polly, in tears. "Why, I couldn't leave the Little Brown House!" Then she looked from one to the other of the five Peppers. "I couldn't leave you, Mamsie. Nor darling little Phronsie. And not one of the boys."

"I know you couldn't," soothed Mamsie. "We'll just write and tell Mr. King we're sorry."

And so she did, with many thanks. But Mr. King was not to be put off so easily. He stormed, fretted, and even begged. He offered every advantage. Polly was growing up, he said, and she should have an education! He would give her the best foundation for a musical education that the city could afford. She would also have lessons in the schoolroom of his house under the boy's private tutors.

Polly lifted her head with pride.

"It is wonderful that Mr. King wants to do all this for me," she said, "but we just couldn't accept that much. Now, could we, Mamsie?"

Mrs. Pepper was very proud, too.

"No, we couldn't," she answered. "It's different the way Mr. Henderson teaches Ben at home."

So, for a second time, they wrote their thanks to Jasper's father.

Almost in the very next mail, another letter came from him. Now Mr. King was really angry. By being so stubborn, Polly was making Jasper ill! In fact, he had been ill for weeks, but they hadn't told the Peppers. Didn't they even care, the letter asked angrily, if he were sick or well?

Now this was a different case, entirely, declared Mrs. Pepper. To her independent soul, to take, and not to give was a sin. If Jasper needed Polly, she'd have to go!

And soon all of Badgertown knew that pretty Polly Pepper was going to the big city! Many brought her farewell gifts, and that made her sad.

If the truth were told, Polly had never been so sad in all her life. How could she ever, ever leave the Little Brown House! It had been her home since the day she was born. To leave it and Mamsie and the other little Peppers — oh, she couldn't! She just couldn't.

Finally Mrs. Henderson told her:

"But don't you see, Polly, that you will help your mother twice as much as you possibly could here by getting a good education? Think what your music will be! Only think, Polly!"

But Polly drew a long breath and turned away from the minister's wife.

Then Ben spoke in a choking voice.

"Oh, Polly, if you give this up, there'll never be another chance." He put his arm around her and whispered something in her ear.

"I know," said Polly quietly, and then she burst out, "but I can't. It isn't right!"

Then Mrs. Pepper did something the children had never seen her do before — she burst into tears!

"Polly," she said softly, "I think my heart will break if you don't go. It will mean so much to you all the rest of your life."

"Oh, Mamsie!" cried Polly, flinging herself into her mother's arms. "I'll go — if you think I ought to."

Living In A Big House

POLLY had delayed the stagecoach for so long that it was time for the train to start as soon as it reached the railroad station. The stage driver put her under the care of the railroad conductor. Almost before she knew it, the whistle blew on the locomotive and she was riding along mile after mile of silvery tracks.

She sat up very straight among her many bundles. Her suitcase had been placed at her feet, and Cherry was on the seat beside her, hopping about in his cage. There were also bundles of things that wouldn't go into the suitcase.

Several hours flew by before she could count them. Then, as the train rounded a curve, she saw the rooftops of a city.

People on the train began to bustle about. They wanted to be sure to get off before it started on to another station. The wheels ground to a stop. Even before the conductor could come and help Polly, she heard a boy's voice:

"Polly! Polly! Polly!" And there beside her stood Jasper!

"Oh, hello! Hello!" Her face became very bright and her voice was a happy cry. "I just didn't believe you'd be able to come to the train to meet me!"

Jasper laughed gaily.

"The minute I knew you were really coming, I began to get better, Polly, so I just hopped out of bed."

He picked up her bundles and gave her suitcase to a porter. Then they started to walk to where a handsome carriage waited at the station. Mr. King was standing beside it, fussing and fuming as always.

"Why wasn't the train on time?" he grumbled. "I had to look all over the place for a porter." Then suddenly he discovered Polly and his scowls were replaced by smiles. He gave her a big hug.

"Bless me, Polly," he began, "you're the sweetest sight in the world! I'm so glad you're here, I could sing!"

Soon she was helped inside the carriage. It was lined with dark green satin and had many cushions. She felt like a princess.

Through the heart of the city, down narrow, noisy streets they were driven. Finally they were out on a broad avenue with stately mansions on either side, and sweeping lawns and gardens between them.

"Oh!" said Polly, startled at this elegance.

"What is it, my dear?" asked Mr. King.

She drew a deep breath.

"You live here?" she asked hesitantly.

"Yes, of course," said Jasper's father. And Jasper added, "Why not?"

And then the carriage turned in at a brownstone gateway. It wound among fine old trees and stopped in front of a house so beautiful that it reminded Polly of a castle in Ben's book of fairy tales. A butler stood at the front door, stiff and attentive, and then —

Well, children just seemed to tumble right out of the front door! There were Van and Dick and Percy, who was ten years old. They all called, "Polly! Polly! Polly!" even before she could reach them. There was such a sincere welcome in their eyes that she felt, as she said afterward, "happiness all over."

Behind them came their mother, the charming Mrs. Whitney. She led Polly into the house and up a broad winding staircase. It had a carpet so thick that one could sink into it, Polly told Mamsie later. Still a bit shy, in spite of her welcome, Polly held on to Mrs. Whitney's hand.

"Now, Polly," said Mrs. Whitney, "I'm going to have you right next to my own dressing room. This is your home and I hope you'll be happy." Suddenly she gathered Polly into her arms. "You just don't know how wonderful it is going to be for me to have a little girl! I'm already in love with you, Polly."

Polly would never forget the first time she saw her pretty blue bedroom.

And all the rest of that day she became familiar with room after beautiful room. She sat at the handsome dining-room table made elegant with candle-light. She watched quietly moving servants answer every call. Then, thinking of Mamsie tending table in the Little Brown House, her eyes grew suddenly misty. What were her own loved ones doing? What were they eating in their shabby kitchen?

Jasper showed her the green-house. Here many plants and cut flowers were grown just for family use. He picked a golden jonquil for Polly and tucked it in her hair. Then he showed her the carriage house where Prince came bounding from a corner.

"Oh, Prince! Prince! Where have you been?" Polly rushed forward to embrace him happily.

While the big dog nuzzled his furry face right against hers and licked her cheek with his pink tongue, Jasper explained: "I had to keep him tied up until now. Father said to wait until you got settled before I let him bowl you over!" Then he added gaily. "You may come with us now, Prince. We're going to show Polly the schoolroom."

She liked the schoolroom at once. It had a big blackboard, a desk for the teacher, and an American flag. It also had four desks, one for every boy in the house. Then Jasper pointed to a new one.

"That's for you, Polly," he grinned. "I guess you'll study hard."

"I certainly will," she said very soberly.

"And now," said Jasper, "there's something else."

He led her through the house again into the beautiful parlor. Polly stood stock-still.

"Oh!" she breathed softly, and just stood and looked at a black ebony piano. "Oh, lovely, lovely, lovely!" She barely breathed the words while Jasper laughed and said:

"Here's where you will learn music."

And Polly did. A French music teacher came the very next morning to give her lessons. Here and in the schoolroom, she worked so hard to learn well, that even Mr. King had to tell her:

"Take things a bit easy, Polly, my child. Don't work so hard that you'll make yourself sick."

She didn't tell him that she was trying so hard to learn things just to help Mamsie and the little Peppers. So she kept at it. But one day as she practiced on the piano, Polly let go.

Tears filled her eyes. She bowed her head over the white ivory keys. Finally she whispered only to herself:

"Everything is wonderful here. I love everyone in this house. We have such fun, the boys and I, but, oh, I keep seeing the Little Brown House and wanting my Mamsie and all the Peppers!"

Polly was as sick as Mr. King feared she would be. Polly was *homesick!*

The Peppers Look Ahead

M<small>RS. WHITNEY</small> looked at Jasper's father.

"You can't really blame Polly for being homesick," she said. "She's never been away from that Little Brown House in her life."

"Well, she can't go back," he grumbled. "I want her to stay here."

"Then what can we do?" asked Mrs. Whitney, thinking of Polly lying upstairs longing for Mamsie, Phronsie and the boys. "I love her just as much as you do, but we just can't have her grieving."

Mr. King got out of his chair and started pacing the room.

"I can't say I blame her," he said gruffly. "I have never seen people nicer than the Peppers or any so happy with so little. And it *is* little, Marian." Suddenly he turned to face her, as though he had solved the whole problem. "I know what to do now! We'll send for Phronsie as a surprise for Polly."

A few days later, Phronsie arrived. Mr. King himself met her at the railroad station, carrying a new doll as flaxen-haired as she was. Then he took her home to Polly. And such a reunion he had never seen! Then Mrs. Whitney and all the boys fell in love with Phronsie, too. She was the new little queen of the big house.

Not only did Mr. King assemble a whole family of dolls for her, he took her almost everywhere he had to go. Then a strange thing happened. Mr. King — Jasper King — became afraid! He had never been afraid of anything in his life, but he was now. He feared that Mrs. Pepper and the boys back in the Little Brown House would miss Polly and Phronsie so much, they would send for them to come home.

He spoke to Mrs. Whitney sadly:

"I just know it will happen," he said, "and we can't allow it. I am going to ask all the Peppers to come here for a visit."

"All the Peppers!" she echoed.

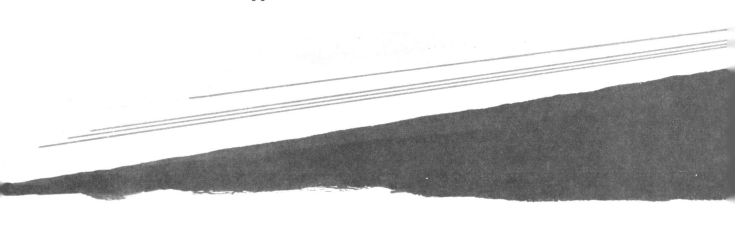

"It's the only way," said Mr. King. "They'll never be happy apart."

When Jasper heard that his father was sending for Mamsie and the boys, he ran as fast as he could to tell Polly. He found her in the hall with Phronsie. The little girl had been playing a game she had named "Upstairs." This meant she would climb the big oak staircase to the top, then turn around and come down again! Polly feared that climbing so much would make Phronsie tired, but the little girl only clutched her doll more closely and said:

"Once more, Polly! Just once more!"

Then Jasper came racing out of the library.

"Polly!" he called. "What do you know? We're sending for your Mamsie!"

"Mamsie?" Polly's eyes were bright at once.

"Mamsie!" repeated Phronsie and stood as still on the staircase as a little golden-haired angel.

Before the great day came, Jasper, Polly and the boys decorated the

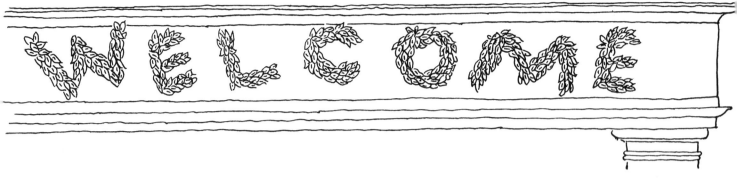

whole house. They even made a "Welcome!" sign out of laurel leaves and hung it above the library door. Then they drew a picture of the Little Brown House so that it would seem the Pepper family had never left it.

On the day that the rest of the Peppers were expected to arrive, the children put fresh flowers in every single room. Polly had said that Mamsie loved flowers. Then they all waited until she and the boys stepped out of Mr. King's carriage right in front of the house. Polly and Phronsie flew into Mamsie's arms.

"My dears! Oh, my dears!" cried Mamsie. "Why, you're knocking off my bonnet! What will Mrs. Whitney think?"

Mrs. Whitney came forward.

"I think this is a very happy day for me, too," she said, smiling.

So their visit began. Ben and David and Joel became friends with the Whitney boys. It was as though they had known each other all their lives. As for Jasper, he felt like a king! To think that all the Peppers were here — right here in this house — the best friends he had ever had! And Prince seemed happy, too. Everywhere the children went, he went along with them.

Then one day Mrs. Pepper said:

"It has all been wonderful, but now we must go home. We cannot impose on the Kings any longer."

And Jasper's father, hearing her, bellowed:

"Just what do you mean, impose! Now I have a word for you, Mrs. Pepper." He laid down his newspaper and looked at his sister who was sitting nearby. "Soon your husband will be home and you and Van and Dick and Percy will be leaving here, won't you?"

Marian looked anxious.

"Yes, I'm afraid we will," she said.

Then Mr. King stood up and looked down at Mrs. Pepper.

"I'll be all alone," he said. "Jasper and I — all alone in this house. I'll have to have a housekeeper." Suddenly his grim voice softened. "I want you to stay and keep house for me with all the Five Little Peppers."

Mamsie looked stunned.

"But — but — " she stammered.

"No 'buts' at all," said Mr. King in his usual gruff way. "The children must all have an education and now it's all settled. You'll all be together while they get one."

And so it was settled, indeed. They would move from the Little Brown House into this mansion in the city! Jasper was so happy that he turned cartwheels the whole length of the hall! Even Prince seemed to smile. But Polly's eyes grew misty.

"The Little Brown House will be sad," she said. "It will miss us very much."

Mamsie laid her hand on Polly's shoulder.

"I think," she said comfortingly, "that the Little Brown House will know why we're leaving and it will give us its blessing."